For my lovely sister, Anita
—L.P.

For Evie and her mommy and daddy
—C.P.

Text copyright © 2018 by Lou Peacock

Jacket art and interior illustrations copyright © 2018 by Christine Pym

Visit us on the Web! rhcbooks.com

Educators and librarians, for a variety of teaching tools, visit us at RHTeachersLibrarians.com

Library of Congress Cataloging-in-Publication Data is available upon request.

ISBN 978-1-9848-4769-0 (trade)

ISBN 978-1-9848-4770-6 (lib. bdg.)

ISBN 978-1-9848-4771-3 (ebook)

The text of this book is set in 18-point ItsaSketch.

The illustrations were rendered in watercolor, colored pencils, and potato stamps.

MANUFACTURED IN CHINA

10 9 8 7 6 5 4 3 2 1

First American Edition

Toby
is a
Big Boy

by Lou Peacock

illustrated by Christine Pym

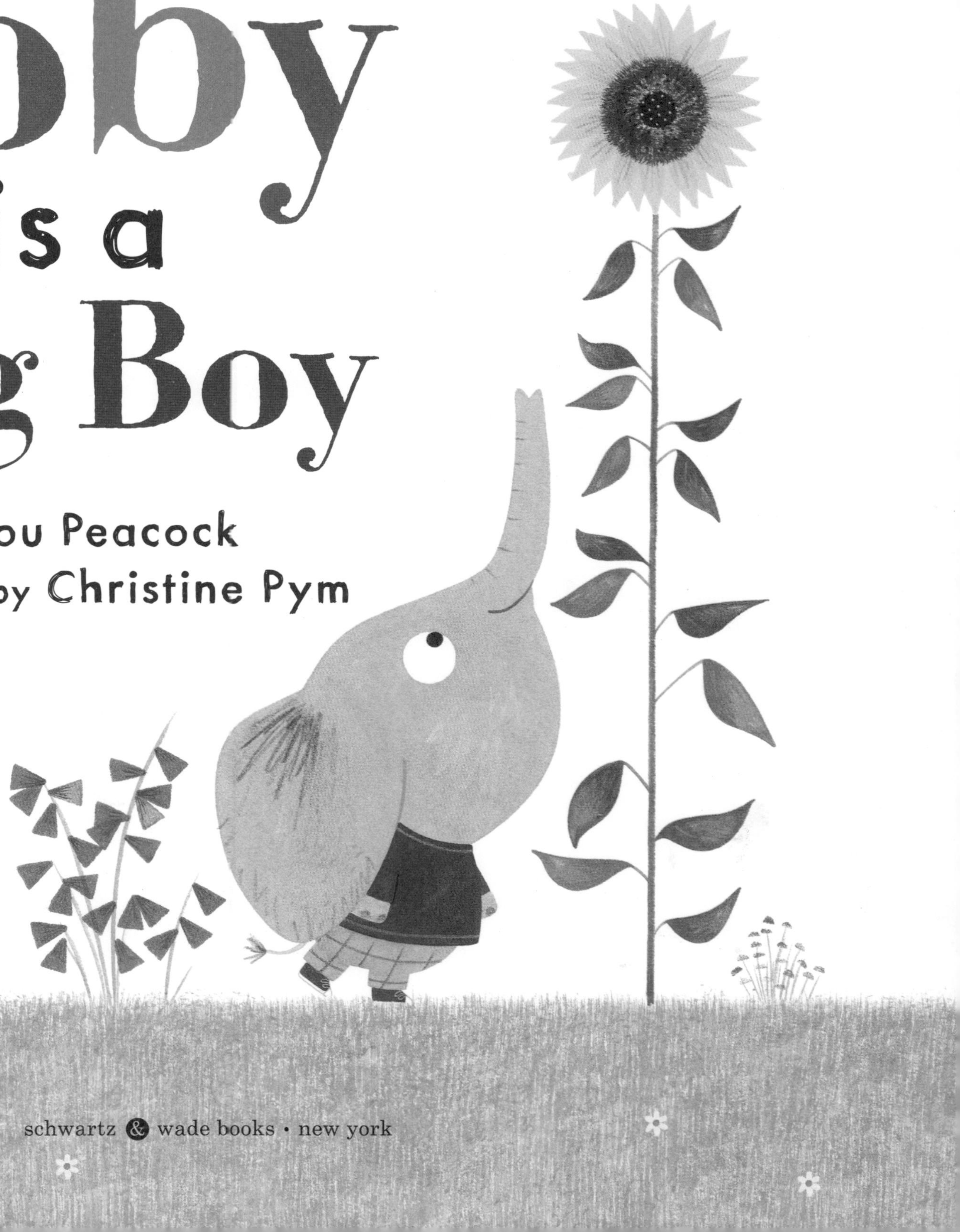

schwartz & wade books • new york

Toby knew that
he was getting bigger.

He thought he might
be a big boy.

He could pour
his own milk.

He could read his own
bedtime stories.

He could even reach the snacks that Mama said were "just for mamas."

In fact, he could do most things **All By Himself.** Being a big boy, thought Toby, was exciting.

He was also bigger than
his little sister, Iris.

Iris was very,
very small.

And because Iris was so small,
Mama was very busy.

Sometimes it felt like Toby
had to do everything
All By Himself.

Even the hard things.

When Toby had to do up his buttons,
Mama was too busy with Iris to help.

"I'm just putting Iris's hat on, Toby," she said.
"But you're my big boy. You can do things All By Yourself."

But Toby couldn't,
and his coat was crooked all day.

When Toby had to put on his rain boots,
Mama was still too busy with Iris to help.

"I'm just putting Iris in her stroller, Toby," she said.
"But you're my big boy. You can do things All By Yourself."

But Toby couldn't,
and his rain boots
didn't match all day.

And it was VERY hard
to go potty
All By Himself.

Toby began to wonder
if being a big boy wasn't
so exciting after all.

He called for Mama . . .

"Mama, pants and toilet paper
are too hard for me," Toby said.
"I can't do everything All By Myself."

"Toby, you are such a big boy and you
can do a lot of things All By Yourself,"
said Mama, "but I can always help you."

Just as Toby began to feel better,
Iris started to cry and Mama had to go.

Toby was mad.

I will show Mama what I can do
All By Myself,
he thought.

He packed a suitcase.
Then, when everything was ready,
he set off **All By Himself.**

Toby opened the door to
the backyard All By Himself.

He climbed

down the steps

All By Himself.

And then he sat
on his swing . . .

All

By

Himself.

Toby was soon
hungry and cold.

Toby didn't feel like
being a big boy
anymore.

Being a big boy
wasn't exciting.

But just at that moment . . .

"Toby!" said Mama.
"There you are!
Why did you walk off like that?"

"I don't want to be a big boy," sniffed Toby.
"I want to be a baby like Iris."
"Oh, Toby," said Mama. "Iris can't do all the exciting things you can do.

But however big
you are, and even when
you're all grown up . . .

you will always be my baby."
"Always?" said Toby.

"Yes," said Mama. "Always."